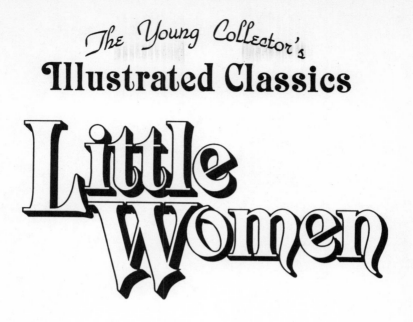

The Young Collector's
Illustrated Classics
Little Women

By
Louisa May Alcott

Adapted by
Devra Newberger Speregen

Illustrated by
Richard Lauter

Cover Art by Ned Butterfield

Copyright © 1995 Masterwork Books
A Division of Kidsbooks, Inc.
3535 West Peterson Avenue
Chicago, IL 60659

Manufactured in the United States of America

Contents

THE MARCH SISTERS

The four March sisters, Meg, Jo, Beth, and Amy, sat around the fire, waiting for their mother to come home.

"Christmas won't be Christmas without any presents," grumbled Jo.

Meg put down her knitting. "It's so dreadful to be poor!" she sighed.

"Some girls have so many pretty things, while others have nothing," sniffed Amy.

"But we have Father and Mother

and each other," Beth reminded them.

"But we haven't *got* Father," Jo pointed out. "And we won't have him with us for a long time."

Nobody spoke for a moment, thinking about how their dear father had gone off to the Civil War. Too old to fight, he'd gone as a chaplain.

Though the March family was poor, they were very happy. Their house was plain and simple, but a cozy, warm place just as well.

Christmas was just a few days away. Each girl had been promised a dollar to spend any way she liked. But there were to be no presents this year, their mother had told them. She believed they should not spend money on pleasure when so many men were suffering a cold winter at war.

Margaret, or Meg, was the oldest sister. At 16, she was pretty and fair-skinned, with large eyes and blonde hair. She stared down at the old dress she

was wearing. "How I wish there was a new dress for me this Christmas," she said sadly.

Fifteen-year-old Jo, or Josephine, was the second oldest sister. She was tall with long, thick brown hair. "I would buy myself some new books," she said. Jo loved to read.

"And I would buy some sheet music," said Beth from her chair in the corner. Beth, who was 13, was very shy and loved music.

"What about you, Amy?" asked Meg.

Amy smiled and tossed her long curls. "I would buy a nice big box of drawing pencils!" she declared. Everyone knew that the youngest March daughter loved to draw. In fact, she was very talented.

The girls returned to their knitting. It grew quiet in the cozy room as they each thought of how they would spend their dollar. Outside, the cold December snow fell, while inside the warm fire crackled.

The clock struck six and reminded them that their mother would soon be home. Suddenly, they all had the same idea. They would each buy something for their mother with their money.

"Slippers!" suggested Meg.

"And new shoes!" cried Jo.

"And a set of handkerchiefs," Beth added.

"I'm going to buy Marmee some cologne," Amy said.

Just then, the girls heard their mother walk through the front door.

"Shhh!" Meg whispered. "Let's keep it all a secret and surprise her on Christmas!"

The girls nodded cheerfully and went back to their knitting so Mrs. March wouldn't suspect a thing.

"How nice to find you all so merry!" Mrs. March said when she saw their happy faces.

The girls jumped up to greet their mother and help her out of her wet clothes.

"I've got a treat for you after supper," Mrs. March said, settling comfortably in her warm chair by the fire. "A letter from Father! A nice long letter."

"When is he coming home?" Beth asked hopefully.

"Not for many months, dear," Mrs. March answered sadly. "A year, perhaps."

After supper, Meg, Jo, Beth, and Amy sat at their mother's feet, anxious to hear the letter. It was cheerful and full of news, but everyone sniffed when Mrs.

March came to the end.

"Give them all my dear love and a kiss," Mrs. March read out loud. "Tell them I think of them every day and every night."

When Mrs. March finished reading, nobody spoke. Jo felt a tear drop off the end of her nose. Amy hid her face in her mother's shoulder and sobbed.

A year was certainly a long time to wait.

CHAPTER

A MERRY CHRISTMAS

Jo was the first one up on Christmas morning. There were no stockings hanging at the fireplace. At first she was disappointed, but then she felt something under her pillow. She pulled out a pretty crimson-colored book.

"Meg, wake up!" she cried, shaking her sister's shoulder.

Meg woke to find a book under her pillow, too. Beth and Amy found books as well, and the four ran off to thank their mother.

"Where is she?" asked Meg.

Hannah, the family servant who'd been with the Marches since Meg was born, told the girls that a young boy had come to the door begging for food and that their mother had gone with him to see what his family needed.

"She'll be back soon," Meg told her sisters, "so let's get everything ready."

The gifts were collected and put in a basket. There were gloves from Meg, new slippers from Jo, embroidered handkerchiefs from Beth, and a bottle of cologne from Amy.

The front door suddenly banged open and the girls heard their mother come in.

"There's Marmee! Hide the basket, quick!" cried Jo. The basket of gifts was hidden under the sofa and the girls raced to the breakfast table.

"Merry Christmas, Marmee!" the girls cried out.

"Merry Christmas, my daughters," Mrs. March replied warmly. "But I have something to tell you before we sit down to breakfast. Not far from here is a poor woman with six children and a newborn baby. They have no firewood and must stay in one bed to keep from freezing. They have no food and are very hungry. Will you give them your breakfast as a Christmas present?"

Though they were hungry themselves, the girls gathered up the breakfast feast and set out to bring the unfortunate family some food. When they arrived and saw the pitiful conditions, they worked together to build a fire with the wood Hannah carried, and set the food on the table for the poor children.

Back home, the four sisters presented their mother with the basket of gifts. Beth played the family's old piano as her mother stared at the basket in surprise.

Mrs. March was touched by the sweet presents from her daughters. The slippers and gloves were put on at once, and a handkerchief scented with cologne was slipped in her pocket. But she was especially proud of the thoughtful way her girls had helped the poor family that morning.

The rest of the day was devoted to preparations for their Christmas dinner. But when Hannah called the family to the table, the biggest surprise of all was waiting for them.

The sisters stared at one another in amazement. Sitting on the table were five big dishes of ice cream and a platter of cake and fruit. And in the center of the table were four bouquets of fresh flowers!

Amy's eyes were wide with excitement. "Did fairies do this?" she asked.

"It must have been Santa Claus!" offered Beth.

"Aunt March," Jo said, reminding

them of their father's wealthy aunt.

"No, it was Mother," Meg said know-ingly.

But Mrs. March shook her head. "You're all wrong," she said. "It's from our neighbor, Mr. Laurence."

"The Laurence boy's grandfather!" Meg exclaimed. "But we don't even know him!"

Mrs. March explained that Mr. Laurence had heard about their helping the poor family at breakfast, and sent the treats over in honor of their good intentions.

"I'll bet that boy put the idea in his grandfather's head!" Jo said. "He's such a nice boy, I wish we could get to know him better."

Mr. Laurence and his grandson lived next door in a grand house, but the March girls barely knew them. Everyone said the grandfather kept the boy inside with his tutor, Mr. Brooke, and made him study all the time.

"Our cat ran away once," Jo said, "and the boy brought her back. And I've talked with him a few times over the fence. He's really a nice boy. I'd like to get to know him better. We all should. I think he's lonely. He needs some fun."

Everyone agreed and talked about getting to know the Laurence boy better as they ate their cake and ice cream. Christmas without presents turned out much better than expected.

CHAPTER 3

THE LAURENCE BOY

"Jo! Jo! Where are you?" Meg cried. "We've just been invited to a New Year's Eve dance!"

She waved the elegant invitation over her head joyously.

"Marmee said we may go," she added, "but what shall we wear?"

"Our cotton dresses," Jo answered. "We haven't got anything else!"

"I wish I had a silk dress!" Meg sighed dreamily.

"Your cotton dress will be just perfect," Jo assured her. "But mine is burned in the back."

"Then you must sit still and keep your back out of sight," Meg told her. "I'm going to buy a new ribbon for my hair and ask Marmee to lend me her little pearl pin. My gloves will do just fine, though I wish I had new ones."

"Mine are stained with lemonade, so I'll have to do without," Jo said with a shrug. Jo never fussed or bothered about dressing up.

"Oh, you must have gloves!" Meg exclaimed. "I'll lend you one of mine and we'll each wear one good one and carry one bad one."

On New Year's Eve, Meg and Jo prepared for the gala while their two younger sisters watched in envy. There was a great deal of running around, laughing, and talking.

Finally, they were ready. Meg wore her silver and blue dress with lace frills

and her mother's pearl pin. Jo wore a
maroon dress pinned with a white
chrysanthemum. Each wore one white
glove and carried one stained one. Meg's
high-heeled shoes were tight and hurt
her, though she didn't dare change
them. Jo complained that her hairpins
were sticking into her head.

"If you see me doing anything wrong, just remind me with a wink," Jo said to Meg.

"No, winking isn't ladylike," Meg replied. "I'll lift my eyebrows if anything is wrong. Now, remember to hold your shoulders straight and take short steps."

"Yes, yes," Jo grumbled.

When they arrived at the party, they joined a group of girls, but Jo didn't care much for girlish gossip, so she wandered off. No one came to talk to her, but she couldn't move around too much because of her burned dress.

After standing alone for a while, she finally slipped behind a curtain into another part of the room. She was surprised to find herself face to face with the Laurence boy.

"Oh! Pardon me," she stammered. "I didn't know anybody was in here."

But the boy laughed and said pleasantly, "Don't mind me. Stay if you like."

"Thank you, Mr. Laurence," Jo said cordially.

The boy laughed again. "Please, I'm not Mr. Laurence. I'm only Laurie."

"Laurie Laurence. What an odd name!"

"My first name is Theodore," he explained, "but when some boys began calling me Dora, I made them call me Laurie instead."

Soon they were talking and laughing comfortably. Laurie felt at ease with Jo, and Jo decided she liked the Laurence boy better than ever. She took several long glances at him so that she might describe him to her sisters. He looked about sixteen, had curly black hair, dark eyes, a handsome nose, and he was tall.

Back in the ballroom, Jo and Laurie danced together until Jo noticed Meg waving her over. Jo followed her into another room, where she found her sister on the sofa, holding her ankle and looking pale.

"I've sprained my ankle," Meg said, rocking in pain. That stupid high heel turned and I can hardly stand. How am I going to walk home?"

"I'll ask Laurie," Jo offered. "He can call for a carriage."

"Mercy, no!" Meg cried. "Don't ask anyone. I'll just stay in here until Hannah comes."

Jo left to fetch supper and coffee for Meg and ended up spilling the dark liquid on the front of her dress.

"Oh, dear!" she muttered under her breath. She quickly reached for her glove and scrubbed at the wet stain.

"Can I help you?" a friendly voice asked.

Jo looked up to see Laurie. She explained that she was bringing supper to Meg who had hurt her ankle. Laurie offered to help immediately and arranged for the girls to ride home in his grandfather's carriage.

At home, Meg and Jo tried to slip

into their room as quietly as possible, but as soon as their door creaked open, two sleepy heads popped up.

"Tell us about the party!" Beth and Amy cried eagerly.

Jo had saved some sweets for her sisters which they ate happily, listening to Meg and Jo tell of their exciting evening.

At breakfast the next morning, everyone seemed out of sorts. Meg complained, Jo grumbled, Beth had a headache, and Amy searched frantically for her shoes. Even Hannah was feeling grumpy.

When Meg and Jo put on their coats and prepared to leave for work, Jo was still grumbling. They set out down the path from their front door, then turned to look back. They always looked back after leaving the house. The sight of their mother waving and smiling at them from the window made them more cheerful.

After Mr. March lost his fortune in an effort to help a friend in need, the two girls offered to go to work and earn money to help the family. Meg found work as a nursery governess for a family named King, and Jo had agreed to take care of her father's old Aunt March.

Aunt March was a difficult woman to get along with, but somehow Jo had managed to charm her. She didn't really enjoy having to work for Aunt March, but she certainly did enjoy Aunt March's large library of fine books! The moment Aunt March took her nap each day, Jo hurried to the library to read.

Jo had always dreamed of doing something splendid with her life, but meanwhile, she loved to read, ride horses, and run. However, her quick temper, sharp tongue, and restless spirit were always getting her into trouble.

Beth was too bashful to go to school. She had tried going, but suffered so much that she gave up and decided to take her lessons at home. She did her schoolwork and helped Hannah as much as she could. She also played the family's broken-down piano as much as possible, never too tired to sing for her mother and sisters after a long day's work.

If anybody had asked Amy what the greatest trial of her life was, she would have answered, "My nose." She pinched it and pulled at it, but it always remained rather flat. Amy had a talent for drawing and was happiest when copying flowers and illustrating stories.

While the sisters loved one another dearly, Amy had grown to confide mostly in Meg. Likewise, Beth seemed to favor Jo.

CHAPTER 4

FRIENDS

"Where are you going, Jo?" Meg asked one snowy afternoon as her sister came tramping through the hall in rubber boots and carrying a shovel.

"Out for some exercise!" Jo answered with a twinkle in her eye. For in fact, she had other plans, too. She wanted to call upon Laurie.

"That boy needs to get out and have some fun!" she thought to herself as she put on her coat. "His grandfather keeps him shut up all the time when he needs to be around other young people."

Jo had watched Laurie's grandfather drive away and figured it was the perfect time to call on him. She bundled up, then marched through the snow toward the Laurence house.

A garden and a low hedge separated the March's house from the Laurence's house. The Laurence house was a stately stone mansion with a big coach house and well-kept grounds.

Jo shook her head when she saw Laurie through an upstairs window. "Poor boy," she muttered. Then she had a grand idea. She picked up a handful of snow, formed a snowball and tossed it at the window.

"Hello!" she cried out when she saw Laurie's surprised smile. "How are you?"

"Better," Laurie replied. "I've been shut in with a cold for a week."

"Would you like a nice girl to come over and amuse you?" Jo asked playfully.

"Yes! Please!"

Jo ran to tell her mother, then made her way to the entrance, presenting herself and a covered dish. "From Mother," she said with a smile.

They sat in the big parlor and Jo picked up a book. "Shall I read to you?" she asked.

"Thank you, but I've read all those," Laurie answered. "I'd rather just talk."

"I can talk all day," Jo said with a laugh. "Beth says I never know when to stop!"

"Is Beth the small one who stays at home a lot and sometimes goes out with a basket?" Laurie asked.

Jo nodded.

"The pretty one is Meg," Laurie went on, "and the curly-haired one is Amy."

Jo was surprised Laurie knew her sisters' names.

"I often hear you calling to one another," Laurie explained, "and I can't

help looking over to your house. It's always so lively there. Everyone is so cheerful and your mother seems sweet as well. I haven't any mother, you know," he added sadly.

Jo felt sorry for Laurie. "I just wish you'd come over and see us sometimes. Would your grandfather let you?"

"I think he would, if your mother asked him," Laurie replied. "He's very kind and he lets me do what I like, pretty much, only he's afraid I might be a bother to strangers."

"But we're not strangers," Jo told

him, "we're neighbors! You wouldn't be a bother. We'd love for you to come."

They talked some more, until Laurie mentioned his grandfather's library. Jo's ears perked up at once.

"Come see it," Laurie said.

Laurie led Jo to the library. It was better than Jo had ever imagined. The walls were lined with books and there were pictures and portraits hanging everywhere, and cabinets full of coins and other interesting things.

"What riches!" Jo sighed.

Jo was staring at a portrait of Mr. Laurence when the man himself walked up behind her.

"What have you been doing to this boy of mine?" he asked in a gruff voice.

Jo was startled at first, then saw the twinkle in the gentleman's eye and knew he wasn't angry.

"Only trying to be neighborly, sir," she replied. "Laurie seems a little lonely."

"That's very kind of you, Miss

March. Now, please, won't you join us for some tea?"

Mr. Laurence drank his tea and watched the young people talk. He noticed a change in his grandson—a certain color and life to his face. "She's right," he thought to himself, "the lad is lonely."

Before Jo left, Laurie showed her the drawing room and its grand piano.

"Do you play?" Jo asked.

"Sometimes," Laurie answered.

"Please play now," Jo pleaded. "So I can tell Beth all about it."

Laurie played and Jo listened, thinking of how much her younger sister would love to hear the piano. Before she left, Mr. Laurence invited her to bring her sisters and mother over to visit anytime.

Back home, Jo told her family all about her visit to the Laurence mansion. "We should all be good to him," Jo said, "because he doesn't have a mother. May he visit us too, Marmee?"

Mrs. March smiled a warm smile. "Yes, Jo, your friend is very welcome."

CHAPTER

MR. LAURENCE
AND BETH

Time went on and the Laurence mansion soon became a place where the March sisters felt welcome. And what good times were had! Meg could walk in the conservatory whenever she liked, Jo became quite attached to the library, and Amy copied pictures to her heart's content.

But Beth could not find the courage to go over to the mansion and play the grand piano. She once went with Jo, but

Mr. Laurence had frightened her so with his gruff manner that she ran away. Nothing could convince her to return, until Mr. Laurence himself learned of her fears and set out to mend matters.

He sat in the March's parlor one day and started a conversation about music. "Wouldn't some of your girls like to run over and practice now and then?" he asked Mrs. March. "Just to keep it in tune. They needn't say anything to anybody, just come and go as they please."

Beth took a step forward and pressed her hands tightly together. This was too much of a temptation. "I'll come, if you are quite sure nobody will hear me," she said timidly.

The next day, after a few tries, Beth made her way noiselessly into the drawing room and ran her fingers along the top of the piano. She immediately forgot her fear and sat down to play. She played until dinnertime, when Hannah came to fetch her. Then all she could do was sit at the table and smile. After that, she visited the Laurence's grand piano every day.

A few weeks later, Beth had a wonderful idea. "Mother, I'm going to make Mr. Laurence a pair of slippers. He is so kind to me, I must thank him. May I?"

"Yes, dear," her mother replied. "It will please him very much and be a nice way of thanking him."

Beth wrote a simple note and, with Laurie's help, the note and slippers were smuggled into the old gentleman's study.

The very next afternoon, Beth went out to do an errand. When she returned, she saw the excited faces of her family and wondered what was going on. Her sisters led her to the parlor, and there stood a little piano with a letter addressed to Miss Elizabeth March from Mr. Laurence.

"For me?" Beth gasped, holding on to Jo.

"Yes, just for you! Isn't it splendid of him!" Jo cried.

Beth could barely bring herself to play, she was so excited, but when she did, everyone agreed it was the most remarkable piano they had ever heard.

"You'll have to go and thank him," Jo said jokingly. She didn't think her shy sister would ever go.

But Beth stood at once. "Yes," she said. "I guess I'll go now before I get frightened thinking about it." And to her family's amazement, she walked straight through the garden to the Laurence's front door.

They would have been even more amazed had they seen what she did next. She knocked at the door to Mr. Laurence's study and when he yelled "Come in!" in his usual gruff voice, she walked right in and up to the old gentleman.

"I came to thank you sir, for—" But she forgot her speech and didn't finish. Instead, she threw her arms around his neck and kissed him.

From that moment on, Beth March was no longer afraid of the gruff Mr. Laurence.

CHAPTER 6

JO'S TEMPER

"Jo! Meg! Where are you going?" Amy asked one Saturday afternoon, finding her sisters preparing to go out.

"Never mind," replied Jo. "Little girls shouldn't ask questions."

"Please! Tell me!" Amy wailed. "Can I come with you?"

"I'm sorry, Amy," Meg said quietly. "But you weren't invited."

Amy folded her arms across her chest and pouted. "I know!" she cried.

"You're going to the theater with Laurie! Oh, please let me come, too."

"You can go with Beth and Hannah next week," Meg suggested.

"But that won't be as much fun as going with you and Laurie," Amy pleaded. "Please let me, I've been sick with this cold so long."

Jo cast a stern look in Meg's direction. "If she goes, I won't," she declared. "Laurie only invited us!"

Amy started to cry and was being comforted by Meg, when Laurie called the girls from down below. Meg and Jo rushed down the stairs, but when they got to the front door, Amy called out after them.

"You'll be sorry for this, Jo March!" she yelled in a threatening tone.

Meg and Jo had a wonderful time at the theater, although Jo felt bad about her quick temper with Amy earlier. She wondered what her little sister might do to make her sorry.

When they got home, they found Amy reading in the parlor. Jo took a quick glance around her room to see if Amy had upset any of her things, but everything seemed to be in place.

But the next day, Jo discovered that her journal was missing. She ran downstairs and burst into the parlor.

"Has anyone seen my book?" she demanded.

Meg and Beth said, "No," at once and looked surprised. Then Jo noticed Amy's face turn red as she poked at the fire and said nothing.

"Amy, you've got it!" Jo cried.

"No, I haven't."

"You know where it is then!"

"No, I don't," Amy insisted.

"That's a fib!" Jo cried, giving her a shake. "You know where it is and you better tell me at once or I'll make you!"

"You'll never see your silly old book again!" Amy cried suddenly. "I burned it!"

Jo gasped. "You burned it? My book with all my writing in it?"

"Yes! I told you I'd make you pay for yesterday—" Amy got no further, for Jo began to shake her until her teeth chattered.

"You wicked, wicked girl! I'll never forgive you for this!" Jo ran from the room in a rage.

Jo's book was the pride of her heart. The stories and fairy tales she'd written and rewritten over and over had filled its pages. Amy's bonfire had burned up several years worth of work.

When the bell rang for tea, Jo appeared looking so miserable, Amy asked for forgiveness.

"I shall never forgive you," Jo replied sternly. She ignored Amy for the rest of the evening.

The next day, Jo was still angry. She decided to ask Laurie to go skating to help cheer her up.

Amy heard Jo gathering her skates and wished she could go, too.

Meg put her arm around her younger sister and whispered in her ear. "Go after them," she said. "Don't say anything until you see Jo is in a better mood. Then do something kind and I'm sure she'll make up with you."

"I'll try," Amy said hopefully.

It wasn't far to the river, but both Laurie and Jo had their skates on by the time Amy reached them. Jo saw her and turned her back. Laurie didn't see her, since he'd skated on ahead to test the ice. As he turned around the bend, he shouted back to Jo.

"Keep near the shore," he warned. "It isn't safe in the middle."

Jo heard him, but Amy was struggling with her skates and didn't hear a word.

Laurie was already around the bend and Jo had skated up to the turn, when a strange feeling came over her. She turned around just in time to see Amy throw up her hands and crash through the thin ice.

"Aaaahhhhh!" Amy screamed.

Jo felt her heart stop beating. She tried to call Laurie but her voice was gone. She tried to go to Amy but her feet

wouldn't move. Laurie suddenly flew past her and yelled, "Bring a pole! Quick, quick!"

How she managed it she did not know. But while Laurie lay flat on the ice, holding Amy up by his arm, Jo pulled a pole off a nearby fence and dragged it onto the ice. Together, they rescued Amy from the freezing water.

Shivering, dripping, and crying, Amy was bundled in Laurie's coat and rushed home. In no time, she fell asleep

before the warm fire.

Jo had hardly said a word. She was pale and very shaken. Later, she fell into her mother's arms and wept.

"It's my dreadful temper!" she sobbed. "If she had died it would have been my fault!"

Mrs. March comforted her daughter. "It was an accident, my dear," said Mrs. March. "But you must remember this day and resolve never to have another like it.

You know, my temper used to be even worse than yours," she said. "However, I have learned to keep it in check. Your father helped me. He's a very patient man."

Jo stared into her mother's eyes and thought about her father. Then she looked over at Amy, who lay sleeping by the fire. "What if Amy had died?" she wondered in horror.

Amy stirred in her sleep and Jo ran to her side. She hugged her sister warmly. Amy smiled and hugged Jo back.

CHAPTER

THE CHANGE
IN MEG

In April, Meg's friend Annie Moffat invited her for a two-week visit. The Moffats were very wealthy and fashionable, and the more Meg saw of Annie's pretty things, the more envious she became—and the more she wished she were rich, too.

Meg's sisters helped her pack her trunk for the trip. There were going to be several small parties and a large party on Thursday night. Meg packed her fancy white cotton dress for the occasion.

Though she was nervous at first, the Moffats were kind people and put her at ease. After a few days, Meg began to fit right in, imitating Annie and her friends and putting on airs. She knew if her mother and sisters could see her they wouldn't approve. But she just wanted to know what it felt like to be rich, if only for a few days.

On the night of one of the small parties, Meg, Annie, and several of Annie's friends were getting ready. Meg unpacked her cotton dress. She noticed one of Annie's friends glance at it, then whisper to the other girls. Meg felt her cheeks burn.

Then the maid came in with a box of flowers.

"Oh, it must be for my sister, Belle," Annie cried. "Her fiancé always sends her some."

"No, they are for Miss March," the maid said. "And there's a note as well."

All the girls surrounded Meg as she read the note. The flowers were from Laurie! Meg folded the note and slipped it into her pocket. She felt much better and enjoyed herself at the party. She didn't know why, but the next day, Annie's friends took more of an interest in her. They told her they'd sent an invitation to Laurie for Thursday's party.

Meg laughed when they told her. "Laurie is only a young boy," she said. "A family friend." But the girls all exchanged looks just the same.

Annie's sister offered Meg her blue silk dress for Thursday's party. On Thursday evening, Annie and her sister helped Meg dress up in style. They laced her into the dress, crimped her hair, and lent her earrings and high-heeled boots.

"I'm afraid to go down, I feel so strange," Meg whispered to Annie. But she acted the part of a young society lady perfectly, though her side ached from the tight dress and she kept tripping over the train.

Meg was flirting and laughing with some of the gentlemen guests when she saw Laurie staring at her in surprise. "I'm glad you came," she said to him, speaking in an odd, grown-up voice.

"Jo wanted me to come and tell her how you looked," Laurie replied. "But I don't know what to tell her. You look so...different."

"Don't you like me dressed up this way?" Meg asked.

"No, I don't," was Laurie's blunt reply.

Meg gasped. This was too much, coming from a boy younger than she. She stormed away.

Soon after, someone tapped her shoulder. It was Laurie.

"Please forgive my rudeness and come dance with me," he said. "I don't like your gown, but I do think you are still beautiful."

"Laurie," Meg whispered as they danced, "please do me a favor and don't tell them at home about my dress. I feel so foolish. I thought it might be fun to dress up and act fashionable, only I'm sure people are just staring at me, talking about how silly I look."

Laurie agreed not to tell.

The next day, Meg felt sick from drinking too much champagne at the party. On Saturday, she went home, and home seemed wonderful—even if it wasn't fashionable and rich.

Meg told her family of her adventures and said she'd had a charming time. But later, she confessed to Jo and her mother that she had allowed the Moffat girls to dress her up, and that she had made a spectacle of herself flirting and drinking too much champagne.

She also told them about some gossip she'd overheard concerning Laurie. Meg said some girls mentioned that Mrs. March had plans to set Laurie up with one of her daughters because he was rich.

"Rubbish!" cried Jo.

Mrs. March agreed that she did not have any such plans for her daughters.

"I want my daughters to be beautiful and good, to be admired and respected, to lead useful lives, and to marry only for love and happiness."

CHAPTER 8

THE EXPERIMENT

"The first of June!" Meg cried out happily. "The Kings are off to the seashore tomorrow and then I'm free for three whole months!"

Jo smiled at her sister. "I have vacation, too," she said. "Aunt March left this afternoon."

"I'm going to sleep late and do nothing!" Meg sighed.

Jo glanced at the pile of books at her side. "I'm going to sit in my favorite apple tree and read every day."

Amy turned to Beth. "Why don't we put away our lessons for awhile and take some time off, too?" she suggested.

"If it's all right with Mother," Beth replied. "I'd love to learn some new music."

The girls all turned to their mother, who sat sewing in what they called "Marmee's Corner."

Mrs. March smiled. "You may try your experiment for a week and see how you like it," she told them. "I think that by Saturday night, you will find that all play and no work is as bad as all work and no play."

"Oh, dear no!" Meg exclaimed. "I think we shall find it wonderful!"

The next morning, Meg did not get out of bed until ten o'clock. She ate breakfast by herself, and she noticed the room felt lonely and untidy, for Jo hadn't bothered to straighten up as she usually did. Beth had not dusted and Amy's books lay scattered about.

Meg finally took a seat in Marmee's Corner and read, while Jo left to go rowing with Laurie. Beth cleaned out her closet, and Amy left, with her easel in hand, to do some painting.

At teatime, they compared notes and all agreed that it had been a delightful, though unusually long day. Meg discovered she'd ruined her favorite blue blouse in the wash, Jo had a sunburned nose and a headache, Beth's closet was unfinished and a mess, and Amy had ruined her dress after getting caught in a rain shower. Still, they assured their mother that their experiment was working well.

The long days passed slowly and by Friday night, no one would admit that they were tired of the experiment. Then, on Saturday, Mrs. March gave Hannah the day off. When the girls woke up and came down for breakfast, there was none.

"Mother isn't sick, only tired," Meg told her sisters. "She's going to spend the day in bed, resting."

Then Jo got an idea. "I'll make dinner, so Mother won't have to!" She ran to invite Laurie, and when she returned, Meg shook her head. "You'd better see how it turns out before inviting company." She knew Jo wasn't much of a cook.

By the time Jo began preparing for dinner in the kitchen, the rest of the March household was in a state of confusion. Beth was crying over her pet canary, Pip, who had died overnight, Meg was entertaining a guest in the parlor, and one of their thin, gossipy old neighbors paid them a call, reminding

them she'd been invited for dinner that evening.

The dinner Jo served that night became a standing joke among the family. She overcooked the asparagus, burned the bread black, didn't buy enough seafood for everyone, and under-cooked the potatoes.

When everyone was seated, Jo wished she could crawl under the table as she watched her banquet go uneaten.

Amy giggled, Meg looked distressed, the neighbor pursed her lips, and Laurie chuckled.

Then Jo remembered dessert. "Well, at least I couldn't possibly have ruined that!" she thought to herself. She took to the table a big bowl of fresh fruit and a pitcher of rich cream for topping. Everyone smiled as she portioned it out in pretty glass dishes. It wasn't until Laurie took the first bite that Jo began to worry all over again.

"What is it?" Jo asked.

Laurie's mouth puckered slightly, then Amy choked out loud and hid her face in her napkin.

"Salt instead of sugar," Meg replied quietly, so as not to embarrass an already mortified Jo.

Jo groaned and fell back in her chair. She was on the verge of crying, when she happened to catch sight of Laurie's puckered face. Suddenly, it all struck her as hilarious and she began laughing as tears rolled down her face. Soon, everyone else was laughing, too— even "Croaker," which was what they called the old neighbor. The unfortunate dinner ended gaily, with a merry feast of bread, butter, and olives, things Jo hadn't had to cook.

Later, Mrs. March asked her daughters how they liked their little experiment. "Would you like to continue it for another week?" she said.

"Not me!" Jo cried out.

"Or me!" echoed the others.

"Lounging doesn't pay," Jo declared. "I'm going to spend the rest of my vacation learning something useful," she added.

"How about cooking?" Mrs. March asked. Then everyone broke down in gales of laughter all over again.

CHAPTER 9

CAMP LAURENCE

Spring came, and the girls filled their days with gardening, long walks, rows on the river, and flower hunts.

As a friendly gesture, Laurie thought it would be fun to set up a post office for the two families. It was made from an old birdhouse in the hedge between the two houses.

He was right, for the post office was tremendous fun, as well as very useful. Everyone used it, even Mr. Laurence.

Beth was elected post mistress, since she was always at home. She liked her new job of distributing the mail.

One day, Jo received a note from Laurie, inviting her and her sisters to a picnic at Longmeadow with himself and a few of his friends. Laurie's tutor, Mr. Brooke, would also be there.

The sun shone brightly the next morning and promised a fine day. The girls hurried out of bed to prepare for the big picnic. Amy had slept with a clothespin on her nose, in the hopes that it might change shape over night, which made her sisters laugh.

Beth peered out the window and reported what was going on next door. She saw a carriage of people arrive and urged her sisters to hurry.

Laurie met them downstairs and introduced them to his friends. The party was soon ready to board two boats. Mr. Brooke and Ned Moffat rowed one boat, while Laurie and Jo rowed the other.

Meg sat facing Mr. Brooke. He was a grave, silent young man, with handsome brown eyes and a pleasant voice. Meg thought he was very smart and though he didn't talk much, he stared at her a great deal.

By the time they reached Longmeadow, everyone seemed to be getting along quite nicely.

"Welcome to Camp Laurence!" Laurie joked as he climbed onto shore. When the boats were all unpacked, he suggested a game of croquet.

Afterwards, they had lunch, and a very merry one it was.

"There's salt here, if you prefer," Laurie joked, as he handed Jo a plate of fruit.

"Thank you, but I prefer spiders," Jo replied, picking out two that had fallen into the pitcher of milk. Then they all laughed.

When lunch was over, they played some more games, then Mr. Brooke, Meg, and Kate—the older group—sat apart. Kate took out her pad and sketched, while Mr. Brooke lay on the grass with a book.

"Do you like teaching?" Meg asked Mr. Brooke.

"Yes," he replied. "It's easy when you have a pupil as bright as Laurie. I shall be sorry to lose him next year when he leaves for college."

"Then what will you do?" Meg asked.

"As soon as he leaves," Mr. Brooke explained, "I will become a soldier. Go where I am needed again."

"I should think every young man should want to go where he is needed," Meg declared. "Only it's very difficult for the mothers and sisters who stay home," she added sorrowfully.

A few more games, another croquet match, and a great deal of conversation

later, the afternoon came to an end. At
sunset, the tent was taken down, the
hampers packed, the boats loaded and
the whole party floated down the river
singing at the top of their lungs.

CHAPTER 10

SECRETS

When the fall came, Jo hid away in the attic, her special place where she did all her writing. When she finished her manuscript, she took it and another one from her desk, crept downstairs and out the door.

She walked at a fast pace to the city until she reached a certain street. For awhile, she stood in a doorway, calming her nerves before finally going up the stairs.

When Jo came back downstairs ten minutes later, she looked as if she'd been through a trying ordeal. Laurie was waiting for her. He had seen her leave in a determined manner and decided to follow.

"Why are you here alone? Are you up to some mischief, Jo?" he asked. "I have a secret to tell," he added, "but first you must tell me why you're here."

"What's your secret, Teddy?" Jo asked. She and Laurie had become such close friends, she'd taken to calling him Teddy. Jo was the only one Laurie let call him that.

"Yours first!" Laurie insisted.

"But I haven't got any," Jo said.

"Oh, yes you do, Jo! You never could keep a secret. Now 'fess up! Then I'll tell mine."

"Promise you won't make fun of me, or tell anyone at home?" Jo asked.

Laurie nodded.

"Well, I've left two stories with a newspaper man and he's going to tell me if he likes them next week."

"Hurrah for Miss March!" Laurie cried. "The celebrated author!"

"Please, stop," Jo asked. "It probably won't come to anything. But I at least had to try. Now, tell me your secret."

Laurie looked around, then leaned in and whispered in Jo's ear. "Mr. Brooke has Meg's glove!" he said. "Isn't that romantic?"

"How do you know?" Jo asked, not pleased with the information.

"I saw it in his pocket," Laurie replied.

"This is awful," Jo groaned. "I wish

you hadn't told me. I don't like the idea of anyone interested in Meg." Lately, Jo had felt that Meg was becoming a woman, and she dreaded the separation she knew was soon to come.

For the next two weeks, Jo behaved so strangely that her sisters wondered if she were ill. She rushed to the door when the postman rang, was rude to Mr. Brooke, and whispered a lot to Laurie.

One Saturday, as Meg sat sewing, she heard shrieks of laughter coming from the yard. A few moments later, Jo ran in with a newspaper and fell on the couch pretending to read.

"What are you reading?" Meg asked.

"Oh, just a story," Jo replied.

"Well, why don't you read it out loud for all of us to hear?" Meg suggested.

Jo cleared her throat and read the romantic tale. Her sisters all listened intently and Meg even cried at one part.

"That was beautiful," Meg said. "Who wrote it?"

Jo jumped off the sofa and tossed the paper in the air dramatically. "Your sister!" she shrieked.

"You?" Meg cried, dropping her sewing.

"It's very good," Amy commented.

"I knew it! I knew it!" Beth chirped. "Oh, Jo, I'm so proud!" She ran to hug her sister.

Meg grabbed the paper from the floor and read the name underneath the article. "Miss Josephine March, it says!"

she cried. "I can't believe it!"

Mrs. March was proud of her daughter, too, and Jo watched excitedly as her family passed the newspaper around, each wanting to see her name in print. Then she took a deep breath and told them how she gave the story to the man in the city, then waited two agonizing weeks for his answer.

When her breath finally gave out, Jo tossed the paper in the air again, and fell back on the sofa crying tears of joy.

CHAPTER 11

A TELEGRAM

November came and the girls agreed it was the most disagreeable month in the year.

Meg was at the kitchen table when Mrs. March came in and asked her usual question, "Any letter from father, girls?"

Before Jo set off for the post office to see about the letter, there was a sharp ring at the door. Seconds later, Hannah came in with a telegram. Mrs. March snatched it, read it, then dropped back into her chair. Jo took it from her and read aloud in a frightened voice.

MRS. MARCH:

YOUR HUSBAND IS VERY ILL. COME AT ONCE TO WASHINGTON.

The room became incredibly still. "I shall go immediately," Mrs. March said quietly. "I hope it's not too late."

At first, the only sound in the room was sobbing. But then everyone quickly set about to help Mrs. March get ready. Laurie was to send a telegram and drop off a note at Aunt March's. The money for the sad journey would have to be borrowed. It was decided that Mr. Brooke would escort Mrs. March to Washington.

By the time Laurie returned, everything was arranged. Only Jo was nowhere to be found.

Everyone began to worry, when suddenly Jo burst in and laid a roll of bills before her mother. "That's my contribution towards making Father more comfortable and bringing him home!"

Mrs. March was stunned. "My dear, where did you get twenty-five dollars?" she asked. "I hope you haven't done anything rash."

"No, it's mine, honestly," Jo replied. "I didn't beg, borrow, or steal it. I only sold what was my own."

As she spoke, she removed her bonnet and everyone could see that her hair—the long hair she'd always been so proud of—had been cut off. An outcry rang out and Beth ran to tenderly hug her sister's cropped head.

"It was nothing, really," Jo said, trying to sound casual. "It feels so much lighter."

But her family wasn't fooled. "What made you do it?" asked Amy, who would just as soon cut off her head as her pretty, long locks.

"I wanted to do something for Father," Jo answered. "As I was passing the barber shop, I noticed the hair pieces and asked if they bought hair. Without stopping to think, I asked him what he would give me for my hair."

Mrs. March was overcome by her daughter's selflessness. No one wanted to go to bed, but by ten o'clock, Mrs. March insisted. Beth played her father's favorite hymn on the piano before the girls went silently up to bed.

Meg lay awake for a while after her sisters fell asleep, but suddenly she heard a stifled sob. She leaned over and touched her sister's cheek, only to find it was wet with tears.

"My hair," Jo sobbed into her pillow. "I know it's vain and selfish of me, but I can't help it."

"Poor Jo," comforted Meg.

The next morning, they awoke before dawn and ate breakfast in silence. Mrs. March's trunk was packed and waiting in the hall by the door. When the carriage came, the sisters kissed and hugged their mother with all their might, then waved as she rode away.

They watched as the carriage disappeared down the street. Jo hung her head and went into the kitchen. "I feel as if there's been an earthquake," she said sadly.

"It's as if half the house is gone," Meg added.

In the days following, news about their father comforted the girls. He was dangerously ill, but the presence of his wife had already done him some good. Mr. Brooke sent a message every day and they became more and more cheerful as each week passed.

Everyone was eager to write, and plump envelopes often jammed the March's postbox, waiting to be taken to Washington.

CHAPTER 12

DARK DAYS

A week after their mother had left, the girls' daily routine finally fell back into place. They were concerned for their father, but sure that with their mother to look after him, he'd be all right.

Ten days after Mrs. March's departure, Beth tried to get one of her sisters to go with her to visit poor families as her mother had done. "The Hummel baby is sick and I don't know what to do for it," she told them. Beth had been to visit the Hummels every day and watched helplessly as the baby became sicker and sicker.

No one could find the time to go, so Beth slipped into the chilly air and went alone.

Later, Jo went upstairs and found Beth sitting on the medicine chest looking very grave and ill.

"What's the matter?" Jo cried.

"Oh, Jo, the baby's dead!" Beth sobbed. "It died in my lap while I was holding it. Scarlet fever!"

"How dreadful!" Jo said, taking her sister in her arms. "I ought to have gone instead of you. I had the fever already, and so did Meg. Oh, Beth, if you should become sick, I could never forgive myself!"

"Don't be frightened," Beth replied. "I shan't have it too badly. I took some medicine and I feel better already."

But Jo stared at her sister and knew she wasn't being honest. Beth's cheeks were flushed and her forehead

was hot to the touch.

"I'll get Hannah anyway," Jo said.

Hannah told the girls not to worry. She called Dr. Bangs to come see about Beth, then sent Amy off to stay with Aunt March so she wouldn't catch the fever.

Amy flew into a rage at having to stay with her aunt. She declared she'd rather have scarlet fever than go to Aunt March's house. Finally, she agreed to go when Laurie stepped in and promised to come and take her for a ride every day.

Dr. Bangs said Beth had the symptoms of scarlet fever, but they all decided not to tell Mrs. March. She couldn't leave Father anyway and it would only make her worry. Still, Meg felt guilty when she wrote to her parents and didn't mention Beth's illness.

Beth was much sicker than anyone but the doctor and Hannah suspected. She slept a lot, and sometimes didn't even recognize her sister's faces when she was awake. Jo devoted herself to taking care of Beth day and night.

With Beth so sick and Mother and Amy gone, the house seemed dark and lonely. Laurie haunted the house like a restless ghost, and even Mr. Laurence locked the grand piano because he couldn't bear to be reminded of his young neighbor who used to play for him.

Everyone missed Beth. The milkman, baker, grocer, and butcher asked about her, and all the neighbors sent comforts and good wishes.

The first of December was a wintry cold day and the snow fell fast. When Dr. Bangs came that morning, he looked at Beth and said, "If Mrs. March can leave her husband, she'd better be sent for."

Jo raced out and sent a telegram. "I've sent for Mother," she told Laurie when she returned.

Laurie's face turned white. "Oh, Jo,

it's not so bad as all that?" he cried.

"Yes, it is," Jo managed to reply. Then tears began to stream down her cheeks. With a lump in his throat, Laurie held out his hand to comfort her.

"I'm here, Jo. Hold onto me. Keep hoping for the best. Your mother will be here soon and everything will be all right. I telegraphed her yesterday, and she'll be here tonight."

Jo stared at Laurie in shock. She dried her eyes, then threw her arms around his neck. Laurie patted her on the back, then followed it with a bashful kiss.

"Grandpa and I decided it was time

to do something," Laurie told her. "The late train comes in at 2:00 a.m. I shall go for her."

"Thank you, Teddy!" Jo cried. "Thank you!"

For the rest of the day and through the evening, Meg and Jo hovered over Beth. The hours seemed to drag by. The doctor came to check on Beth and said that some change would take place around midnight.

When the clock struck twelve, all was still the same with Beth. An hour later, Laurie left for the train station.

It was past two when Jo, who was staring out the window thinking of how dreary things were, heard movement by Beth's bed. She rushed quickly to Beth's side and cried out when she saw her sister.

A change had most definitely taken place. The fevered flush and look of pain were gone. Hannah ran to Beth's side as well and reached out to touch the young girl's forehead.

"The fever has broken!" she cried joyfully. "She's sleeping naturally. Praise be given!"

Before the girls could believe the happy truth, the doctor came and confirmed it. Meg and Jo held each other close.

"If only Mother would come now," Jo prayed.

Soon after, there was the sound of bells at the door below and Laurie's voice cried out. "Girls, she's come! Your Marmee is home!"

CHAPTER 13

A RING FOR AMY

While everyone was caring for Beth, Amy was having a difficult time at Aunt March's. Aunt March watched over everything Amy did. As the days passed, Amy felt more and more like a helpless fly caught in the web of a very strict spider.

In addition to Amy's many chores, Aunt March also insisted Amy read aloud to her every day after dinner. If it hadn't been for Laurie's daily visit and

Aunt March's old maid, Esther, Amy felt she could not have gotten through the dreadful ordeal.

Esther befriended Amy and let her examine all the pretty things in Aunt March's house—the big wardrobes, the ancient chests, and the many cabinets full of interesting things such as velvet cushions and jewelry.

"I wonder where all these pretty things will go when Aunt March dies," Amy said to Esther one day as she examined one of her aunt's jewel cases.

"To you and your sisters," Esther replied. "It is in her will."

"How nice!" Amy said. "But I wish she'd let us have them now."

Esther shook her head. "It is too soon, Amy. But I happen to know that the little turquoise ring will be given to you when you go home."

Amy's eyes widened. "Do you think so?" she asked excitedly. "I'll be very good if only I can have that ring! I do

like Aunt March after all," she added.

From that day on, Amy was a model of obedience. She was very excited about the turquoise ring and imagined how grand she'd look wearing it on her finger.

But when Laurie had come and said that Beth was in danger, Amy closed her eyes and prayed for her sister. As her heart ached, she felt that a million turquoise rings would not make up for losing a sister.

When Beth finally woke from her

long sleep, the first person she saw was her mother. Too weak to speak, all she could do was smile before falling back asleep.

Meg and Jo listened to the news about Father and Mr. Brooke as they and Mrs. March sat by Beth's bedside.

Laurie went off to keep Amy posted of Beth's condition. But he fell asleep on Aunt March's sofa after the tiresome night and didn't wake until he heard Amy's shouts.

"Marmee!" Amy cried joyfully at the sight of her mother.

As Amy and her mother sat talking, Mrs. March noticed the turquoise ring on her daughter's finger.

"Aunt March gave me the ring today," Amy explained. "I'd like to wear it to remind me not to be selfish. Beth isn't selfish, so I'm going to try and be like Beth. May I?"

"Wear your ring, dear," Mrs. March replied, "and do your best. Now I must get back to Beth. We will soon have you home again, little daughter."

That evening, Jo slipped into Beth's room and found her mother. "I want to tell you something, Mother," she said seriously.

"What is it, dear?" Mrs. March asked, holding out her hand to Jo. "Is it about Meg?"

Jo nodded, surprised how her mother had guessed. She sat down at her mother's feet and began to explain.

"Last summer Meg left a pair of gloves at the Laurences' and only one was returned. We'd forgotten all about it until Teddy told me that Mr. Brooke had it. Teddy saw it and teased him about it, then Mr. Brooke confessed to Teddy that he liked Meg but was afraid to say anything because he was so young and poor."

"Do you think Meg cares for John?" Mrs. March asked.

"Who?" Jo asked in confusion.

"Mr. Brooke. Your father and I call him John now. He's been very devoted to us since we've been in Washington. He was very open about his feelings for Meg. He told us he wanted to marry her. He is truly an excellent young man, but I will not consent to Meg marrying so young. But don't say anything to Meg," Mrs. March added. "I don't know whether she loves John yet. I will be able to judge better when I see them together."

Jo wasn't very happy with this new information. Her worst fears were coming true—Meg and John were in love and he would soon marry her and take her away from the family!

"Meg is only seventeen," Mrs. March said. "Your father and I have agreed that Meg shall not marry until she is twenty. If she and John truly love each other, they can wait."

CHAPTER 14

TOGETHER AGAIN

Peaceful weeks followed. As Christmas neared, both invalids improved. Mr. March wrote that he would shortly be home with them, and Beth was soon able to be taken downstairs to lie on the sofa.

On Christmas morning, Beth was carried to the window to see the stately snow-maiden Laurie and Jo had made for her during the night. Then Laurie ran ceremoniously around the house, distributing Christmas gifts. A bed jacket for Beth, a book for Jo, a framed picture for Amy, a silk dress for Meg, and a pin for Mother.

"I'm so full of happiness that if Father were here, I couldn't hold another drop!" Beth declared joyfully. Jo then led her into the study to rest.

Half an hour later, Laurie opened the parlor door and popped his head in very quietly. In a breathless voice he announced, "Here's another Christmas present for the March family!"

There in the doorway was a tall man, leaning on the arm of Mr. Brooke. For several seconds, nobody spoke. Then Amy jumped up and embraced the tall man.

"Father!" she cried as tears ran down her face.

The rest of the family surrounded Mr. March. Jo nearly fainted and had to be tended to by Laurie. Amy sobbed on her father's boots. And Mr. Brooke,

caught up in all the excitement, kissed Meg in front of everyone.

Then the study door flew open and Beth ran straight into her father's arms.

There was never such a Christmas dinner as was had that night. Mr. Laurence, Laurie, and Mr. Brooke dined with the Marches in honor of the home-coming. After dinner, the family sat around the fire.

"Just a year ago we were groaning about Christmas, remember?" Jo asked.

"It's been a rather rough road for you to travel," Mr. March told his daughters, "but you have got on bravely." Mr. March praised each of them—Meg for her hard work, Jo for how ladylike and gentle she'd become, Beth for not being as shy as she used to be, and Amy for her new, unselfish manner.

Then, for the first time in many months, Beth sat at her little piano. "This is a song I wrote for Father," she said, softly touching the keys. And in her sweet, melodic voice, Beth ended the wonderful evening with a song.

The next day, Mr. Brooke called on Meg. When Jo heard his voice at the front door, she whispered to Meg, "I believe he's come to propose to you."

Meg felt her stomach jump. "Well, if that is true," she said, trying to sound casual, "I will tell him very calmly, 'Thank you, Mr. Brooke, you are very kind, but I agree with my parents that I am too young to get married.'"

But when Mr. Brooke came into the parlor, Meg panicked. She stared hard at her sewing and couldn't bring herself to look up at him.

Mr. Brooke approached Meg and took her hand. "I won't trouble you, Meg," he said warmly. "I only want to know if you care for me a little. I love you so."

This was the moment for the calm, proper speech, but Meg just hung her head. "I don't know, I'm too young," she said in a shaky voice.

At that moment, Aunt March came hobbling into the room. She had heard Mr. March was home and rushed over.

"Bless me, what's this?" she cried after seeing Meg and Mr. Brooke together.

"It's Father's friend," Meg stammered. "I'm...uh, so surprised to see you."

"That's evident," Aunt March replied after Mr. Brooke left the room. "What mischief are you up to, Margaret? I insist you tell me right now! Do you mean to marry this man? If you do," she added, "not one penny of my money will go to you!"

Meg folded her arms across her chest. "I'll marry whom I please, Aunt March," she said.

"Highty-tighty! Is that the way you take my advice? It's your duty to marry well and help your family. But I see you intend to marry a man without money, position, or business. I thought you had more sense."

"We are willing to work," Meg cried, "and we mean to wait! I'm not afraid of being poor. I know I shall be happy because he loves me."

Aunt March was very angry. She had had her heart set on making a fine match for her pretty niece. "Well, I wash my hands of the whole affair! I'm disappointed in you, Margaret. Don't expect anything from me when you're married!"

She slammed the door in Meg's face and drove off. Mr. Brooke suddenly reappeared.

"I couldn't help hearing, Meg," he said breathlessly. "It proves you do care for me!"

"Yes, John," Meg whispered.

Soon after Aunt March's departure,

Jo came downstairs to find her sister sitting on Mr. Brooke's knee, looking blissful. The scene made Jo gasp and stop dead in her tracks.

"Sister Jo, congratulate us!" Mr. Brooke cried.

Jo felt a lump form in her throat. This was too much! She ran upstairs and told the awful news to her family. Only they didn't share in Jo's sentiments. They were very happy to hear about Meg and John.

Later, Laurie came to the house with a huge bouquet for "Mrs. John Brooke." Everyone listened as Mr. Brooke spoke of his love for Meg.

Jo took a deep breath and glanced around the room at the happy, loving faces of her family. She saw the tender way Mr. Brooke looked at her sister.

Her heart slowly began to warm at the idea of Meg getting married. After all, she'd still have her older sister around for three more years.

CHAPTER 15

THE FIRST WEDDING

The three years that passed brought few changes to the family. The war ended, and Mr. March came home for good.

John Brooke joined the army for a year, then prepared to work to buy a home for Meg.

Meg spent her time working and waiting. She and John sat together in twilight every night, talking over their plans and dreaming about their future.

Jo never went back to work for Aunt March. The old lady had taken a fancy to Amy and offered her drawing lessons in exchange for taking Jo's place. So Jo devoted herself to her writing and to Beth, who remained delicate long after the fever had passed. Jo still wrote short stories for the newspaper, but dreamed of someday writing more important stories.

Laurie went to college to please his grandfather, but he played more than he worked. Often, he brought home the fellows from his class, and Amy became quite the favorite among them.

The Dovecote was the name of the tiny, charming house Mr. Brooke prepared for his and Meg's first home. It had simple furniture, plenty of books, flowers on the windowsill, and pretty gifts made by the sisters.

Jo and Mrs. March helped Meg set up the new house. Hannah prepared the kitchen, and Amy's artistic talents were helpful with the decorating. Even Aunt March, who had had a change of heart, stocked the new linen closet for her niece.

Meg's wedding took place on a beautiful June day. When she awoke, her heart was filled with excitement.

"I don't want to look strange or fixed up today," she told her sisters. "I wish to look like my familiar self."

So she wore a wedding gown she'd made herself, and the only ornaments she wore were lilies of the valley, John's favorite flower.

"You do look like our own dear Meg," Amy cried, "only so sweet and lovely that I would hug you if it wouldn't crumple your dress!"

"Then I am satisfied," Meg replied. "But please hug and kiss me, everyone, and don't mind my dress." She opened her arms and hugged all her sisters at once.

There were to be no ceremonious

performances. Everything was to be as natural and homelike as possible.

A silence fell as the young couple took their place under the green arch. Mother and sisters gathered close, and when the time came, Meg gazed straight into her husband's eyes and said, "I will!"

After a simple luncheon of cake and fruit, people strolled through the house and garden. Laurie began a festive dance and soon everyone was promenading down the path.

The little house was not far away, and the only bridal journey Meg took was the quiet walk with John from the old house to the new. When she appeared in her new suit and bonnet, she said a bittersweet good-bye to her sisters.

They stood watching, with faces full of love and hope, as Meg walked away with her new husband and her arms full of flowers.

And so began Meg's married life.

CHAPTER 16

ARTISTIC ATTEMPTS

Amy tried her hand at all types of art. She devoted herself first to pen and ink drawing, then oil painting, then charcoal portraits. After this, she experimented with plaster casts, until one day they found her hopping around with her foot stuck in a pan of hardened plaster. With much difficulty and some danger she was dug out, but Jo was so overcome with laughter, she cut Amy's foot by accident.

Meanwhile, Amy was learning and doing other things as well, hoping to become an attractive and accomplished woman, even if she never became a great artist. And she had indeed succeeded, for she was well-liked and had many friends.

One of Amy's weaknesses, however, was her desire to be part of the best society. Money, position, and elegant manners were of the highest importance to her.

Jo, on the other hand, had no

interest or patience for such things. But, like Amy, Jo was very talented and creative. Her art was her writing, and she was a promising author indeed.

Every few weeks, Jo would shut herself up in her room, put on her "scribbling suit" and fall into a "writing frenzy." When the "writing frenzy" came on, she would stay up there all day, writing her heart out.

During these times, her family would keep their distance until Jo emerged—usually tired, hungry, and cross.

One evening, Jo attended a lecture. She arrived early and sat next to a young, studious lad who was reading a newspaper. The lad noticed Jo watching him and offered her half his paper.

"Want to read it?" he asked. "It's a first-rate story."

Jo accepted and soon found herself engrossed in an engaging story of love, mystery, and murder.

"Pretty good, eh?" the lad asked.

Jo shrugged. "I think you or I could do as well if we tried," she replied.

"I would feel pretty lucky if I could!" the lad exclaimed. "The author of this story makes a good living from writing. She knows what folks like and gets paid well for writing it."

The lecture began, but Jo couldn't keep her mind on it. She copied down the address of the paper and resolved to try for the hundred-dollar prize offered for the most sensational story. By the time the lecture ended, Jo had already written most of the story in her head.

She said nothing of her plan at home, but fell to work the very next day. She sent it off to the newspaper and waited for six weeks. She was just about to give up hope, when a letter arrived, along with a check for one hundred dollars. Jo cried out in happiness.

Of course, her parents and sisters were proud of Jo, and when the story was published everyone read and praised it.

"What will you do with such a fortune?" Amy asked her sister.

"Send Beth and Mother to the seaside for a month or two!" Jo answered promptly.

To the seaside they went, and back to her desk Jo went. She wrote several more stories and earned several more checks that year. Thanks to her efforts, Jo was able to buy a new carpet for the house and dresses for her sisters.

Then Jo decided to submit her

novel to three publishers. One publisher contacted her and after she'd promised to cut it down a third, it was published. For this, Jo earned three hundred dollars.

CHAPTER 17

MEG'S DOMESTIC EXPERIENCES

Meg was determined to be a model homemaker right from the start. One thing she wanted to do was keep her storeroom stocked with homemade preserves. So she undertook the task of making her own currant jelly. The currants on their bush were ripe, and John brought home little jelly pots and sugar.

Meg spent a long day picking, boiling, straining, and fussing over her jelly, but it just wouldn't jell. At five o'clock, she sat down in her topsy-turvy kitchen and wept.

It was on this day of all days that John decided to bring a friend home for dinner unannounced. When they arrived at Dovecote, there was not a soul around the house. John rushed in, alarmed by the smell of burned sugar.

John found Meg in the kitchen, sobbing dismally. There was jelly everywhere—on the stove, on the floor, and on Meg.

"Oh, John," Meg wailed, "I'm so tired and hot and cross! I've been at it till I'm all worn out."

"Has anything dreadful happened?" John asked anxiously.

"Yes," sobbed Meg. "The jelly won't jell and I don't know what to do!"

John laughed, then told Meg he had brought a friend home for dinner.

Meg gasped and fell back into her chair. "A man to dinner and everything in a mess! Take him away at once! I can't see him and there isn't any dinner. I hadn't time to cook anything."

"Don't fret, Meg," John said calmly. "We'll pull through and have a good time yet. Just give us cold meat and bread and cheese. We won't ask for jelly!" He meant it as a joke, but Meg didn't think it was funny. Angrily, she fled to the bedroom.

When Meg came down from the bedroom the men had already left. John came home after seeing his friend off. Then the husband and wife both sat, each waiting for the other to apologize first.

"Oh, dear," Meg thought to herself, "married life is very trying." But then she decided she would say "forgive me" first, and walked slowly across the room. She leaned over and kissed John softly on the forehead.

John gazed solemnly at his wife. "It was terrible of me to make fun of you," he said. "I never will again!"

The year rolled around, and in midsummer Meg had twins—a boy and a girl. When Laurie came around to congratulate the happy couple, Jo decided to play a trick on him. She carried her niece and nephew wrapped in one blanket and told Laurie to close his eyes and hold out his arms.

Laurie did, and was only expecting to see one baby when he opened his eyes.

"Twins, by Jupiter!" he exclaimed. "What are their names?"

"The boy is John Laurence," Amy told him, "and the girl Margaret, after Mother and Grandmother. But we shall call her Daisy, so as not to have two Megs."

"Name him Demijohn and call him Demi for short," Laurie suggested eagerly.

"Daisy and Demi!" Jo exclaimed. "That's perfect! Let's tell Meg and John."

And so the babies were known as Daisy and Demi from then on.

CHAPTER

18

CALLS

"Come, Jo, you promised to make calls with me today," Amy said. Jo hated calling on people and never did so until Amy forced her to. But she finally gave in and got up to get dressed.

"Put on your best things," Amy instructed. "Do your hair the pretty way. Take your light gloves and the embroidered handkerchief."

When Jo passed inspection, the girls set off for the Chesters' home. Amy gave further instructions as they walked.

"Now, Jo, the Chesters consider themselves very elegant people, so be on your best behavior. Just be calm, cool and quiet — you can do it for fifteen minutes."

Jo promised, then took Amy at her word and sat silently throughout the whole call. Amy tried desperately to make Jo talk. Even when Mrs. Chester praised Jo's novel, all Jo did was smile back at her politely.

"What a haughty, uninteresting girl the older Miss March is!" they heard someone say as they left. Jo laughed, but Amy was mortified.

Amy pleaded with Jo to be more sociable at the next house, but she was anxious all the same. She wasn't quite sure just how her sister was going to act.

At the next house, Jo embarrassed Amy, and in dismay, Amy decided she was through giving instructions to Jo.

So at the third house, Jo acted herself and had fun. There were boys there, and Jo joined in the storytelling, then played on the grass with the smaller children.

The last call of the day was to Aunt March's. Jo had wanted to go home, but Amy insisted they go because Aunt March liked the company.

They found another aunt, Aunt Carrol, visiting Aunt March. Jo was in a bad mood, but Amy pleased the older women.

During the conversation, Jo mentioned how she likes to be independent.

"Ahem!" coughed Aunt Carrol, as she cast a sly look at Aunt March.

"I told you so," Aunt March replied. Jo burned with anger.

"Do you speak French, dear?" Aunt Carrol asked Amy a while later. Amy nodded, but Jo said she couldn't bear French. She thought it was a silly language.

Another look passed between the two older ladies. Jo felt as if she might explode at any minute and thought it best to end the visit. She shook hands with her aunts, then watched as Amy kissed them both good-bye.

A week later, a letter came from Aunt Carrol.

Mrs. March told the girls that Aunt Carrol was going to Europe next month.

"And she wants me to go with her?" Jo exclaimed, flying out of her chair in excitement.

"No, dear, not you. Amy," Mrs. March replied.

"Oh, Mother! She's too young! It's my turn first—I've wanted it for so long!"

"I'm afraid it's impossible," Mrs. March explained. "Aunt says she'd planned to ask you first, but that 'favors burden you' and that you 'hate French.'"

"Oh, my tongue!" Jo moaned. "Why can't I learn to keep it quiet?"

"Jo, dear," Beth whispered, "I know it's selfish, but I'm glad you're not going. I couldn't spare you."

Jo bore up well until Amy left, then ran up to the attic and cried. Likewise, Amy put on casual airs until the steamer was ready to leave. Then she clung to Laurie and asked him to watch after her sisters.

"I will," he promised. "And if anything happens, I'll come and comfort you," he added, never dreaming he would be called upon for just that.

CHAPTER 19

TROUBLES

"Jo, I'm anxious about Beth," Mrs. March said worriedly. "It's not her health, it's her spirits. She sits alone a good deal and when she sings, the songs are always sad ones. Now and then I see a look on her face that I don't understand."

After sewing thoughtfully for a minute Jo said, "I think it's because she's growing up. Beth's eighteen, but we don't realize it. We treat her like a child." Satisfied that was the reason for the change in Beth, Jo went back to her sewing.

Then, one day, Jo saw Beth sitting at her favorite spot by the window. She was watching Laurie outside and Jo saw a teardrop fall from her eye.

"Mercy on me, Beth loves Laurie!" Jo thought in shock. "I never dreamed of such a thing." Then Jo had a sudden thought. "I wonder if he loves her back? He must! I'll make him!" She couldn't ever bear to see her beloved Beth hurt.

Jo watched Laurie that night. Nothing unusual happened—Beth was her quiet self and Laurie was very kind to her. But Jo's imagination ran away with her and she could swear that Beth was staring at Laurie a little longer than usual and that Laurie seemed more gentle with her younger sister than ever.

In bed that night, Jo was just dropping off to sleep when the sound of a stifled sob made her fly to Beth's bedside.

"What is it, Beth?" she asked anxiously. "Is it the old pain?"

"No, it's a new one. But you can't cure it. There is no cure," Beth sobbed. She clung to her sister and cried so hard it frightened Jo.

"Wouldn't it comfort you to tell me what it is?" Jo asked.

"Not now. Not yet," Beth replied.

"Then I won't ask. But remember Bethy, that Mother and I are always glad to hear and help you."

"I know. I'll tell you by-and-by." Cheek to cheek they fell asleep, and the next day Beth felt a little better.

A few days later Jo told her mother she wanted to go away for the winter. She needed a change and felt restless and anxious. She thought she might go to New York and stay with her mother's friend, Mrs. Kirke, who was looking for someone to teach her children.

"What about your writing?" Mrs. March asked.

"All the better for a change," Jo replied. Then the color rose in her cheeks and she added, "It may be vain and wrong of me to say it, but I'm afraid Laurie is getting too fond of me."

"Then you don't care for him in the way he cares for you?"

"Mercy no! I love the dear boy as I always have, and I am very proud of him, but as for anything more, it's out of the question."

"Are you sure he feels this way about you?" Mrs. March asked.

"I'm afraid so," Jo replied. "He hasn't said anything, but he looks a great deal. I think I had better go away before it comes to anything.

"But Beth must think I'm going to New York to please myself," Jo added, "for I can't tell all this about Laurie to her. But she can comfort him after I'm gone and cure him of this romantic notion."

Mrs. Kirke gladly accepted Jo. The

plans were settled, and trembling with fear, Jo told Laurie. He took the news very quietly, and Jo was relieved. But when he said good-bye, he whispered in Jo's ear.

"It won't do a bit of good, Jo. My eye is on you, so mind what you do or I'll come and bring you home."

CHAPTER

A NEW FRIEND

Mrs. Kirke had a big house and gave Jo the sky parlor with a stove and table. It was the perfect place to sit and write. The two little girls she was to teach were sweet, gentle children.

Soon after Jo arrived she noticed a gentleman border also living at the Kirke's. He had a foreign accent. She later learned from Mrs. Kirke that the man was Mr. Friedrich Bhaer, a professor from Berlin. He was a stout man

with tousled brown hair, a bushy beard, and kind eyes. He looked like a wealthy gentleman, though his coat was missing two buttons and his shoe had been patched.

Jo spent her days teaching, sewing, and writing up in her tiny room. She was finally introduced to Mr. Bhaer one day, then noticed him on her way out a day later. He was standing in his doorway, holding a sock and a sewing needle.

She laughed all the way downstairs, but thought it was sad that he had to mend his own clothes.

One day soon after, Mrs. Kirke called after Jo as she passed Mr. Bhaer's room. "Did you ever see such a room, my dear?" she asked. "Come help me tidy up. I've turned everything upside down searching for the handkerchiefs he asked me to mend."

Jo gazed around the cluttered room. Books and papers were everywhere.

"Such a man!" Mrs. Kirke exclaimed with a laugh. "I agreed to do his washing and mending, but he forgets to leave his things for me!"

"Let me mend them," Jo said. "I'd really like to do it for him. He seems like such a nice man."

When Mr. Bhaer found out, he offered to teach Jo German in return for the mending. It wasn't long before Jo and Mr. Bhaer became good friends. On New Year's Day he gave her a book because he knew how much she loved to read. Not having much money, Jo got him several little things for his room in return for the thoughtful gesture.

Though very busy with her new job with the Kirkes, Jo still found time for her writing. She dreamed of filling her home with comforts, giving Beth everything she wanted, and someday going abroad herself. So she took to writing short "sensation" stories because they paid well.

Jo took one of those stories to a paper called the Weekly Volcano. The editor agreed to publish it, but asked that in the future, she make her stories shorter and spicier. She did, and week after week, her stories appeared in the paper. Her name, by request, never appeared with her stories. She saved the money she earned to take Beth to the mountains next summer.

Jo and Mr. Bhaer became even closer. She respected the professor immensely. One day, during a conversation, Mr. Bhaer said he found the short "sensation" stories in the Weekly Volcano pure trash.

Jo knew deep down that he was right. Of course, Mr. Bhaer hadn't known Jo wrote those stories, for she hadn't told anyone, but she was ashamed just the same. She decided at that moment she wouldn't waste any more time writing such stories.

She went to her room that evening and stuffed all her papers and short story ideas into the burning stove. After that, she never wrote a "sensation" story again.

Jo stayed with the Kirkes until June, when she returned home for Laurie's college graduation.

"You won't forget to come visit, will you?" she asked Mr. Bhaer on the day she was leaving. "I'll never forgive you if you forget, for I want my family to know my friend."

On the ride back home, Jo stared out the window and thought about the past few months. "Well," she said to herself, "the winter's gone and I've written no books and earned no fortune. But I've made a friend worth having and I'll try to keep him all my life."

CHAPTER 21

HEARTACHE

Laurie graduated with honors and the whole March family attended the ceremony along with Laurie's very proud grandfather. Afterwards, Laurie invited everyone to his house the next day for a big celebration. He stared strangely at Jo and asked her if she'd attend. Jo nodded, but was nervous just the same.

The next day she met him on a little path near the river. They spoke for a while, mostly about school and her time in New York. It was uncomfortable and Jo knew what was coming.

She dreaded the moment, then Laurie finally spoke up.

"I've loved you ever since I've known you, Jo!" he blurted out. "How could I help it? You've been so good to me. I can't go on like this any longer."

Jo hung her head and said softly, "I wanted to spare you this. I never meant for you to fall in love with me. That's why I went away. I'm proud and fond of you, Laurie, but I could never love you as you want me to. I can't change my feelings."

"Really truly, Jo?" Laurie asked sadly.

"Really truly," Jo answered.

"Is it because you're in love with that old man?" Laurie asked. "That professor you were always writing home about?"

Jo almost laughed out loud. "He isn't old. He's good and kind and the best friend I've got next to you. I haven't the

least idea of loving him or anyone else!"

"But you will, and then what shall become of me?"

Jo put her hand on Laurie's shoulder. "You'll love somebody else, too, and forget all this."

"I can't love anyone else!" Laurie shouted suddenly. "I'll never forget you, Jo! Never!"

"Yes you will," Jo insisted. This was even worse than she'd imagined. She felt terrible for her friend, but she knew this was all for the best.

"Listen to me, Laurie," she said, "you'll get over this after a while, and find some lovely accomplished girl who will adore you and make a good wife."

Laurie didn't want to hear what Jo had to say any longer. He felt hurt and rejected. So he ran down the path and disappeared.

Jo felt awful and ran after him. Back at his house she found Mr. Laurence and told him the whole dismal story.

Laurie came home after dark and sat at the grand piano. He played a sad, stormy melody, then broke off in the middle.

"I can't stand to see him this way," Mr. Laurence thought. He went into the parlor and comforted his grandson. "You must take it like a man," he told Laurie. "You must get over Miss March. Why not go abroad as you'd planned? Get far away from here."

"Alone?" Laurie asked.

"I'll go with you," Mr. Laurence said. "I have some business in London that needs looking after. I have friends in Paris to visit and you can go on ahead to Italy and Switzerland."

Laurie hesitated. He knew his grandfather hated to travel and that the old man was just being kind.

"As you like, sir," he said with a sigh.

The day arrived when Laurie and his grandfather were to leave. The Marches went to bid them farewell and Laurie embraced them all. He barely hugged Jo before running to meet his carriage.

Jo felt terribly guilty. She stared after him, hoping he'd turn around so she might give him one last friendly wave, but he didn't look back.

CHAPTER 22

BETH'S SECRET

When Jo had come home from New York that spring, she was struck with the change in Beth. A heavy weight fell upon Jo's heart when she saw her sister's face. It was thinner and there was a strange, transparent look about it.

Jo showed her younger sister the money she'd saved, then told her excitedly about her plans for a trip to the mountains. Beth thanked her heartily, but didn't want to go so far from home.

So Jo took Beth to the seashore, where she could let the fresh sea breezes blow a little color into her pale cheeks.

At the seashore, Jo stared at her sister, wondering what was ailing Beth. Then one day, as she looked at Beth's frail sleeping body, she knew. Her sister was dying.

Beth woke to see Jo staring at her and said, "Jo, you know. I tried to tell you but I couldn't. I'm never going to get better. I've known it for a while."

"Is this what made you so unhappy last autumn?" Jo asked.

Beth nodded.

"Oh, Beth, and you didn't tell me! How could you bear it alone?" Jo's heart ached to think of her little sister struggling to say good-bye to health, love, and life.

"I didn't want to frighten you," Beth answered.

"And I thought you were unhappy because you loved Laurie," Jo said.

"How could I, when he was so in love with you?" Beth asked. "I love him like a brother, that's all."

Jo felt the tears that filled her eyes begin rolling down her cheeks. "Oh, Beth, you must get well!" She held her sister tightly as the waves rolled in before them.

"I want to, so much!" Beth told her. "I try, but every day I lose a little more strength." She gazed into Jo's eyes. "You'll tell them when we get back?"

Jo promised she would, but when they arrived home, there was no need for any words. Jo put Beth to bed, then came downstairs to find her father leaning his head on the mantelpiece. He could not bear to turn around when he heard Jo come in. Mrs. March opened her arms to her daughter and Jo ran into her mother's warm embrace and wept.

CHAPTER

23

LAZY LAURENCE

Laurie was in Nice, France on Christmas Day. A carriage carrying a pretty young lady dressed in blue stopped at his feet. He stared a moment, then went to meet her.

"Oh, Laurie, is it really you?" Amy cried in delight. "I thought you'd never come!"

"I promised to spend Christmas with you, and here I am!" Laurie replied.

"I have so much to tell you, I don't

know where to begin," Amy said excitedly. "Get in and we can talk as we drive."

As Amy watched Laurie, she felt a new sort of shyness steal over her. Laurie had changed. He was not the merry boy he'd been. He was handsomer than ever, but Amy thought he looked unhappy and tired.

"Jo writes that Beth is doing very

poorly," Amy said, showing Laurie Jo's latest letter. "I often think I ought to go home. But they say stay, as there's nothing I can do there."

"They're probably right," Laurie agreed.

He had only intended to stay in Nice a week, but Laurie ended up staying a month, escorting Amy to various dinners and parties. The two friends got on beautifully. Laurie was happy to stay. He'd grown tired of wandering around, and Amy reminded him of home.

One day, as Amy and Laurie sat together outdoors, Amy asked, "Laurie, when are you going back to your grandfather? He expects you."

"I only bother him," Laurie replied. "So I thought I'd stay here and bother you a little longer," he added with a wink.

"What would Jo say if she saw you now?" Amy asked, hoping to stir him.

"As usual, 'Go away, Teddy. I'm

busy,'" he replied with a harsh laugh. Amy noticed a new look on Laurie's face —a bitter look, full of pain and regret.

"You are so different," she started to say, but then she stopped. She didn't like him this way at all. And she meant to tell him.

"I have a new name for you," she suddenly announced. "It's Lazy Laurence. How do you like it?"

Laurie stared at her, but his face remained unchanged.

"Do you want to know what I think of you?" she went on.

Laurie's eyes widened, but he said, "Go on."

"Instead of being good, useful, and happy, you are faulty, lazy, and miserable! Here you have been abroad six months and done nothing but waste time and money and disappoint your friends. You have changed since you left home."

Laurie sat and listened as Amy

went on, telling him what he knew was the truth. He felt badly, but couldn't tell Amy the real reason he'd been acting so strange.

That's when Amy suddenly noticed the ring on Laurie's finger. It was a small ring, one that Jo had given him many years ago. All at once, she knew. It dawned on her that Laurie never spoke of Jo. She realized that something must have happened between them.

"What happened with Jo?" she asked quietly.

"I don't wish to talk about it," Laurie replied. "But it's lucky she didn't love me, if I'm the good-for-nothing lazy fellow you say I am." His expression was bitter.

"I was wrong to say that," Amy apologized. "I didn't know. I'm sorry."

Neither of them spoke for several minutes, and Amy was sure Laurie was angry with her.

The next morning, instead of his usual call, Laurie left a short note for Amy. It said that "Lazy Laurence" had gone back to his grandfather. She smiled when she read the note, happy that her message had gotten across.

"I'm glad he's gone," she said with a deep sigh, "but oh, how I shall miss him!"

CHAPTER

24

THE VALLEY
OF THE SHADOW

After a while it became obvious to the family that Beth was not going to get well. They tried to bear it cheerfully. They wanted to make Beth's last year a happy one.

The most pleasant room in the house was set apart for Beth, and in it they gathered everything she loved most —flowers, pictures, her kittens and, of course, her piano. Here she sat every day, trying to keep her spirits up. She continued her sewing, making little presents for her sisters and for the neighborhood children. The first few months were happy ones.

But by-and-by, Beth said her sewing needle was becoming "too heavy" so she put it down. Talking wearied her and her pain grew more intense.

Jo never left her side, not even for an hour. She slept on a couch in the room with Beth, who claimed her older sister's presence made her stronger. Sometimes, when Jo awoke in the night, she found Beth reading or singing softly as slow tears trickled down her pale cheeks.

Spring came and the birds returned, almost as if to say good-bye to Beth. Then, one day, in the dark hour before the dawn, with her mother by her side, she drew her last breath and gave her mother one final, loving look.

When morning came, for the first time in many months the fire was out, and Beth's room was empty and still.

CHAPTER 25

LEARNING TO FORGET

Laurie thought that forgetting his love for Jo would take years, but to his great surprise it grew easier every day. Soon, his feelings for Jo became only those of "brotherly love."

He was still abroad, in Vienna, Austria, when he received a letter from Jo about Beth. Jo asked him to write to Amy often so she would not feel lonely or homesick.

Laurie wrote immediately to Amy, and soon letters flew back and forth

between them. He wanted to visit her in Nice, but he would wait until she asked.

The sad news about Beth's death met Amy at Vevey, Switzerland. She bore it very well, but her heart was heavy and she longed to come home and be with her family.

Laurie was in Germany when he heard the news a week later, and set off immediately to comfort Amy.

When he found Amy, she was alone in a garden, thinking about Beth and why Laurie hadn't come.

When she saw him, she jumped up and ran into his arms. "Oh, Laurie, I knew you'd come to me!"

As they stood together silently, Amy felt no one could comfort her as well as Laurie. And Laurie knew at once that Amy was the only woman in the world who could fill Jo's place and make him happy.

As time went on, Laurie stayed with Amy in Vevey. He didn't have to tell Amy that he'd fallen in love with her. She knew it without words, and she expressed to him that she felt the same way. She knew everyone would be pleased, even Jo.

One afternoon, the two set out for a row on the lake, when Laurie asked her to marry him.

"Yes, Laurie," she answered with a smile on her face and her heart filled with happiness.

CHAPTER 26

ALL ALONE

The days after Beth's death were dark ones for Jo. She was filled with despair at the thought of spending her life alone in that quiet house.

As they sat sewing one afternoon, Jo noticed how happy her sister, Meg, was. She knew having a husband and two wonderful babies made Meg's life content.

"Why don't you write again?" Mrs. March asked. "That always used to make you happy."

"I've no heart to write," Jo replied. "And nobody cares for my writing anyway."

"We do," her mother assured her. "Write something for us. I'm sure it would do you good and please us."

An hour later, her mother peeped in and found Jo scribbling away, with that expression on her face Mrs. March knew all too well.

Jo never knew what got into her that day, for she wrote a story that went straight to the hearts of everyone who read it. Though it was against her will, her father packed up her story and sent it to a magazine, which paid for it and requested others. The story was a major success and Jo received a great deal of praise from friends and admirers.

When Amy and Laurie wrote of their engagement, Mrs. March feared Jo would not be happy for them. Though Jo was quiet at first, she was soon full of hopes and plans for "the children."

"I was afraid you might be hurt by this," Mrs. March said to Jo.

"No, Mother," Jo assured her. "It is better this way. I'm glad Amy has fallen in love with him. I hope they'll be very happy."

Later, Jo was up in the attic, staring at four small wooden chests, lined in a row. Each had the name of a sister carved in front and was filled with relics

from the past. Jo leaned her chin on the edge of hers, and some old notebooks caught her eye. They were from that pleasant winter she'd spent at Mrs. Kirke's.

A small book slipped out from the pile and fell into her lap. It was the book Mr. Bhaer had given her, with a little message written in its cover. Jo stared at his words and they began to take on a new meaning.

"Oh, how I wish he were here," she muttered. Holding the little book in her hands, she laid her head down and cried.

CHAPTER 27

SURPRISES

One evening, Jo sat alone on the sofa, staring into the fire and thinking. Her face looked tired and sad, for the next day was her birthday and she was thinking how fast the years had gone by. She was almost twenty-five.

Suddenly, Laurie's face appeared like a ghost's in front of her own.

"Oh, my Teddy!" she cried joyfully.

"Then you are glad to see me?" Laurie asked.

"Oh, yes!" she replied. "And where's Amy?"

"At Meg's. Your mother and my wife are visiting with Meg and the children."

"Your what?" cried Jo. "You've gone and gotten married?"

"Yes," Teddy said, blushing. "I wanted to be the one to tell you."

Laurie told Jo how the marriage came to be about six weeks before in Paris. "We wanted to surprise you all," he added with a twinkle in his eye. Then he became serious.

"Jo, dear, I want to say one thing, then we'll put it behind us forever. I shall never stop loving you, but the love has changed. Amy and you changed places in my heart. At one time, I didn't know who I loved best, but after I saw Amy in Switzerland, I knew."

Jo hugged Laurie. "My boy has grown into such a splendid man!"

Laurie smiled, but noticed there was a sadness in her eyes. "We all miss

Beth very much," he said. "Poor Jo, you've had a great deal to bear all alone."

"I had Mother and Father with me," Jo said. Then she heard Amy's voice calling from the front door.

"Where is she?" Amy called. "Where's my dear old Jo?"

In trooped the whole family, and everyone hugged and kissed. Amy's face was bright and her voice was tender. Her family could see how happy she was with Laurie. Everyone made a fuss over the two—and over Laurie's grandfather—for they'd all been gone for nearly three years.

They talked and laughed over tea. Then the party, except for Jo, headed into the parlor. She was happy for the young couple, but feeling sad and lonely for herself. Just then, there was a knock at the front door.

Jo opened it and stared as if another ghost had come to surprise her. A tall, bearded gentleman stood in the doorway, beaming at her.

"Oh, Mr. Bhaer, I'm so glad to see you!" Jo cried.

"And I to see you," Mr. Bhaer replied.

"Come in," Jo said at once. "My sister and her new husband have just returned from abroad and we are all very happy."

"Have you been ill, my friend?" Mr. Bhaer asked when he noticed something sad in Jo's manner.

"Not ill, but tired and sorrowful," she answered.

"Ah, yes," Mr. Bhaer said, taking

Jo's hand. "I know. My heart was sore for you when I heard about your sister."

In the parlor, everyone greeted Mr. Bhaer cordially. As he spoke with Mr. and Mrs. March, Jo stole an occasional glance at him. "How wonderful he looks!" she thought, remembering how he mended his own clothes. She stared at his new suit and thought he looked handsome.

When it came time for him to leave, Mr. Bhaer bid everyone a fond farewell. "I will gladly come again, if you will have me," he said to Mrs. March, though his eyes never left Jo. "I have business in the city that will keep me here for a few more days."

Mrs. March said of course, they would love to have him call again, but after he left, Jo wondered what business he had in the city. She would have known, too, if she could see his face as he sat in his room an hour later and stared lovingly at her picture.

CHAPTER 28

UNDER THE UMBRELLA

By the second week of Mr. Bhaer's visit to the city, everyone knew Jo was in love with him, only Jo wouldn't admit it. The change in her was incredible. She sang while she worked, did her hair up three times a day, and had a constant smile on her face.

Every night, Mr. Bhaer came to the March house for a visit. They had wonderful times, talking and telling stories until late. But then he didn't visit for three days and Jo became very cross.

"Gone home as suddenly as he came," Jo muttered one gray afternoon as she prepared for her daily walk. "It's nothing to me, of course, but I should think he would have come and bid us good-bye like a gentleman."

"You'd better take your umbrella, dear," her mother said. "It looks like rain."

"Yes, Marmee. Would you like anything while I'm out?"

Mrs. March gave Jo a list of dry goods she needed, and Jo set out. Soon she felt a drop of rain on her cheek and she realized she'd forgotten to take the umbrella.

She opened her handkerchief and held it above her head as the rain came down harder. Suddenly, a big blue umbrella appeared over her head. She looked up to see Mr. Bhaer.

"We thought you had gone," Jo said, hoping he didn't notice her red cheeks.

"Did you think I would go without

saying good-bye?" he asked.

"No, but I knew you were busy with work. We rather missed you," she added. "Especially Mother and Father."

"And you?" he asked.

"I'm always glad to see you, sir," she replied cooly.

"Then I will come one more time before I leave."

Jo felt her throat tighten. "Then you are leaving?" she asked.

"Yes," he said softly. "I have found work, teaching at a college."

"How splendid!" Jo said.

"Ah, but I fear this college is far away out west."

"Far away," Jo repeated, her heart growing heavy.

Walking home, Jo was sad. It was obvious Mr. Bhaer didn't care for her as much as she did for him. If he did, he wouldn't be going so far away.

Mr. Bhaer noticed the tears in Jo's eyes. "Dearest heart, why do you cry?"

"Because...because you are going away!" she blurted out, much to her embarrassment.

Mr. Bhaer stopped walking and pulled Jo close to him. The rain pelted loudly against the umbrella and on Jo's dress, but she didn't care.

"Jo," Mr. Bhaer whispered, "I came here to see if you could care for me. I wanted to be sure I was more than a friend. Am I?"

"Oh, yes!" Jo cried, embracing him. "But why did you wait so long?"

"It was not easy," Mr. Bhaer explained, "but I could not find the heart to take you from your happy home until I had one to give you myself. Can you be happy with me?"

"Yes," Jo said, reaching up to give him a tender kiss.

For a year, Jo and her professor lived apart, working, waiting, and writing long letters. They met whenever they could. Then, at the start of their second year apart, Aunt March died and left her large home to Jo. She and Friedrich decided to open a school for boys.

Almost before she knew where she was, Jo found herself married and settled in the large house. Soon the school flourished and was filled with boys, both rich and poor.

It never was a fashionable school and they didn't become rich, but it was just what Jo had intended it to be— "a happy, homelike place for boys who need teaching, care, and kindness."

As the years went on, Jo and Friedrich soon had two little boys of their own—Rob, named for Grandpa, and Teddy, a happy-go-lucky baby with his mother's lively spirit.

There were a great many holidays celebrated at the big house, and one of the most delightful was the yearly apple-picking. On a lovely October day five years after Jo's wedding, everyone was there, laughing and singing, climbing apple trees and tumbling down.

For a few quiet moments, Meg, Jo, and Amy sat under a big tree with their mother. Mrs. March gazed warmly at her grown daughters, then stretched out her arms and pulled them very close.

"Oh, my girls," she said with a smile, "however long you live, I never can wish you a greater happiness than this!"

THE END

ABOUT THE AUTHOR

Louisa May Alcott was born on November 29, 1832 in Germantown, Pennsylvania. The second daughter of four, Alcott grew up in a family that had little money. In order to help support her family and make life easier for her mother, Alcott took jobs working as a seamstress, governess, and teacher.

However, writing was the thing that Alcott did best and enjoyed most. In her twenties, Alcott wrote thrillers, poems, and sensational stories—but under a different name.

In 1868, her Boston publisher suggested that she write a novel for girls. With encouragement from her family, Alcott wrote *Little Women*. This book sold millions of copies, and is still very popular.

Alcott continued to write novels for young girls and boys. She died in 1888.

The Young Collector's Illustrated Classics

The Adventures of Robin Hood
The Adventures of Tom Sawyer
Black Beauty
Call of the Wild
Dracula
Frankenstein
Gulliver's Travels
Heidi
Hunchback of Notre Dame
Little Women
Moby Dick
Oliver Twist
Peter Pan
The Prince and the Pauper
The Secret Garden
The Strange Case of Dr. Jekyll & Mr. Hyde
Swiss Family Robinson
Treasure Island
20,000 Leagues Under the Sea
White Fang

Masterwork Classics are available for special and educational sales from:

Kidsbooks, Inc.
3535 West Peterson Avenue
Chicago, IL 60659
(312) 509-0707